THIRTY-TWO

MORE BEARS!

by Kenn Nesbitt

illustrated by Troy Cummings

sourcebooks
jabberwocky

For Ally and Caitie

Published by Sourcebooks Jabberwocky, an imprint of Sourcebooks, Inc.
P.O. Box 4410, Naperville, Illinois 60567-4410
(630) 961-3900
Fax: (630) 961-2168
www.jabberwockykids.com

Library of Congress Cataloging-in-Publication data is on file with the publisher.

Source of Production: Leo Paper, Heshan City, Guangdong Province, China
Date of Production: August 2010
Run Number: 13248

Printed and bound in China.
LEO 10 9 8 7 6 5 4 3 2 1

Once upon a time there was a story.

This story was a lovely story with absolutely no bears in it—not a single bear anywhere. Then one day...

MORE BEARS!!

What? Who said that? The author of the story looked around the room, wondering where those voices had come from. Were those the voices of children shouting? Then he went back to writing.

As I was saying, this story had absolutely no bears at all.
The author was very certain about this.

MORE BEARS!!

The author tried very, very hard to ignore the children who thought that the story ought to have...

MORE BEARS!!

Fine. This story had a bear. It was a cute little baby bear strolling through the book looking for—

MORE BEARS!!

Now hold on a second. The author of this story knew exactly how many bears it should have, and the author insisted there should only be...

MORE BEARS!!

two bears. There. Happy now? An adorable, cuddly-wuddly little baby bear named Mr. Fluffy, and his mama bear, Stella, who always wore a yellow hat. Now it happened that Stella and Mr. Fluffy, like all bears, were especially fond of…

MORE BEARS!!

more bears. Of course. The author was just thinking that. The author was thinking that, just to keep everybody happy, this story should have a papa bear, whose name, by the way, was Captain Picklehead,

and a bear named Uncle Sheldon who was bald and loved to play the ukulele. Now, where were we? Oh, yes...

Stop that! How many bears do you want this story to have, anyway? Do you really want to hear about Bobcat Sam, the bear who rode a pony, and Admiral Haversham, the English dancing bear, and Excellent Steve, the bear who just wanted to surf?

You do? Wow. Why didn't you say so? In that case, the author suddenly decided that what this story really needed was...

Yes, yes, yes. More bears. So the author added Astrobear, who, by the way, was Bulgarian and always kept a hamster in his pocket, just in case. And then the author put in three more bears named Lester, Chester, Ester, and Floyd. Wait. That's four! Oh well, four is okay, because, after all, this story really needed...

MORE BEARS!!

It needed a bear
named Lucky Eddie
who juggled carrots,

and a bear named Elbow who wasn't very smart and always wore his underpants on the outside of his regular pants,

and a bear named One-Two-Three, which even the author thought was a strange name for a bear.

And since this probably wasn't enough, the author added even...

MORE **BEARS!!**

The author added six bears on tiny pink bicycles, two bears reading comic books, one bear flying across the page in a cape and lederhosen, three more bears swinging through trees on vines, a bear in a yellow submarine, several bears making cupcakes, and an entire team of fire-fighting bears running across the page with hoses, ladders, and party balloons.

There were bears hanging from the top of the page, bears sleeping in the corners, and bears standing on top of other bears. There were so many bears in the story that they couldn't all fit on the page.

It was crowded! Too crowded. So crowded that some bears started pushing other bears off of the page. And arguing. Which made the author grumpy. And when authors get grumpy, they start rewriting. Changing the story. In fact, this author was so grumpy he told the bears to leave. And they did. After all, this was the author's story.

They walked off the page. They rode off the page. They swung, surfed, danced, climbed, ran, and even somersaulted off the page.

At last all the bears were gone, and the author smiled. Finally the author had a story with no bears in it. A lovely story with not a single bear anywhere. Just the way the author wanted it. Because, you see, the author was quite certain that this story should have absolutely...